# THE ART OF THE NIGGA

(An In-Depth Guide into the World of the 'New Age Nigga')

Written: Black N.A.T.O.
Inspired By: The *REAL* Niggas

Edited by A'Nonchalant Sallard
Publishing House: ImagineAPlace, llc.

www.imagineaplacellc.com

ISBN 979-8-9855642-2-8

# Dedications

To my environment(s) & to all the good white people who always wanted to say 'Nigga!' in public without any backlash. Here's your license...Say it loud: "Sup My Nigga!"

-T.L. Thomas

To all those who fought to erase the word Nigga from the annals of history. No need to be ashamed...the Real Niggas are alive and, in the flesh, recognize them for who they are & honor them Niggas for all the Nigga shit they've produced!

-O.R. Wilkins

# Acknowledgements

I gotta acknowledge The Sutras of Patanjali (for providing me with the tools to unearth my mental gifts.) To Mr. O. Wilkins for bringing my crazed insights out of the dark and into the Light. To all the White people I've met along this road. I truly understand now. Jah! Ras-Tafari!!!-Mr. T.L. Thomas

--------------------

First, I must say thank you to Mr. Tre'mayne 'Fa$e' Thomas for his willingness to immerse himself into the width, depths, and heights of the world of Nigga-dome. Thank you for being a conscious mind of Reason and Understanding throughout this process. But on the real...you enjoy indulging in that, 'Nigga shit!' It's crazy how you can meet someone and, in a few conversations,Understand...

To my brothers that have strived with me in the Moorish Science Temple...we've grown as Men together, and Allah has blessed us all in our unique way. All (LOVE)! To my brothers who have endured, strived, and thrived with me throughout these 21+ years of perpetual incarceration: Cedric Theus (Thanks for teaching...proofreading...and seeing me as I am. And a plethora of other things we never speak on, never have you told me no, and you've always given me reasonable, rational advice.) Darnell Williams (Hey...it doesn't get any more honest and genuine as you. You see life from a panoramic view...on some MLK shit, but always ready to go, Malcolm, if the situation arises. I can bake better than you though Bro!) Ramale Hunt Sr. (What can I say...we are growing old here. Yet ever since we met some 10+ years ago, your words and your actions have been solid gold!!! I Love your essence.) Bryan Shuford-Bey (From babes 2 Men; running stores 2 running businesses...in due time.) Jerrid Winfrey (I'm so proud of your maturation process! It's crazy how you are setting trends...even while incarcerated.) Damion Seats (I love you lil Bro.; now take yo ass home!!! You got the juvenile life sentence!!! You got an opportunity to go live the shit we've been dreaming about!) Donald Vaughn (Pook...keep pushing and being you.) Reginald Nelson (from the time I met you in the hole, you always have been the same...AN HONEST, LOVING, GOOD-HEARTED NUT!!!) Jason Tate (real talk...you lit a fire under me with that BOL 'Beam of Light Publishing'...Iron sharpens Iron!) It's crazy because...all the above brothers are sentenced to life w/o the possibility of parole, and regardless of what we did, we remain...HUMAN!

To my Ancient Ones: Murray 'Pops' Doss, Steven Frasier-Bey, Doc Lawrence, Jerome Watts-El, Ed Love-El...(The true O.G of this Life without Parole Shit; you all are true MEN...Thank you for showing me, through your actions, how Men are supposed to grow while incarcerated.) Rest In Peace to my Ancient Ones: Simon 'Nefer Em-Ra' Tunstall, Charles Robinson-Bey, James 'Ali' Henderson-El, and James Blair-Bey III (May the Astral Plane welcome you all with open Energy, and may you receive all you deserve for your work on this Plane of things made manifest. ALL LOVE)

Lastly...to all those I've encountered throughout my journey. It was because of the diversity of the Women and Men I've encountered in my 39 years of life (21 of which I've spent incarcerated); that I'm able to produce such a work. So, thank you to all my Real Niggas (of all Nationalities...all genders...all age groups...all religions!) I couldn't have done this without ya'll influence.

Hey Ma & A'Nonchalant...I ain't forgotten y'all. There's no us without the energy that you both give!!! Never forget...The Dynasty is being built, we're the muscle, and you all are...EVERYTHING! Love, Sun.

# Foreword (i.e WARNING)

## THIS IS NOT A HOOD BOOK; NOR IS THIS URBAN FICTION!!!

This is meant to be an EXPERIENCE; plain and simple. For those of you reading this, allow me this OPPORTUNITY to say that, what you've come to BELIEVE about Real Niggas is not true! You see... to KNOW a Real Nigga, one must A.) have a CONSCIOUS EXPERIENCE with a Real Nigga and then B.) Gain an UNDERSTANDING from the EXPERIENCE! Only then will you KNOW what being a Real Nigga is about. Only then will you begin to UNDERSTAND the zeitgeist of this Nigga shit.

So, what does one believe about Niggas and/or Real Niggas? Well, the streets are replete with rumors and ideas about what and who the Niggas and Real Niggas are; as well as what they do. However, until you-the reader-are willing to extricate yourself from the comfort of your environment and visit the world of Niggas, you'll never gain the proper Experience.

So where do you find Niggas and Real Niggas? EVERYWHERE!!! From the crack house to the White House. From Wall Street to Dr. Martin Luther King St. From Africa, all the way to New Zealand; from Maine to Spain, and everywhere in between. Niggas are lurking everywhere. Why? Because being a Nigga was NEVER ABOUT A RACE OF PEOPLE! Being a Nigga was, is, and will always be about an ideology! Plain & Simple.

# Table of contents

# Opening to THE NIGGA BALL

From the slave ships to the Maybach trucks...

Niggers and Niggas have always ridden in luxury.

Black and White alike, with a look in their eyes...

That's that, 'Nigga...you betta not FUCK with me!!!'

From the slave fields to the football fields...

You still see the residue of Niggers acting crazy!

From the White House to the Crack House...

Niggas are running billion-dollar businesses in broad day. These Niggas are brazen!

From the Supreme Court to the Basketball Court...

You'll learn there are Laws to this Nigga shit!

From Rap to Rock n' Roll...

Niggas is pushing out some dope hits!

From International wars to hood wars...

Niggas are killing for no reason!

From aristocrats to hood ballers...

Niggas gone stunt, regardless of the season!

And to ask a Nigga to be anything other than a Nigga...

Well, every Real Nigga knows, that's damn near like treason!

What can I say, welcome one and all! It's our time: NIGGA SEASON!!!

# Chapter 1:
# Lil Jimmy Gets Invited to the Nigga Ball

(Music Playing) *All da Niggas came/from Maine to Spain/reppin' ignance to da fullest/ain't no shame in dey game/Now I'm here to tell ya/Dis here's a hit/Cause in 2023, we on dat Nigga shit...*

"Ah yeah welcome, welcome to the 51st Nigga Ball! (Crowd clapping and cheering) Dis ya girl Maserati ...and I'm ya host for dis extravaganza! We gon'have a ball ta'night! Whassup to all my Real Niggas and Niggarettes in'da build'n ta'night. I see we got some of da Realist Niggas in da build'n tonight! Whassup Suki...you stay on yo Real Nigga shit, kill'n dese Niggas wit dat Good Cat! Reppin' dis Nigga shit fa'real! Oh...whaddup to my nigga Carloss King, kill'n'em wit dat Love and Marriage: Huntsville rich ignant'shit! You out'dere got dem ole Bitches o'dn on dat Nigga shit! Oh shit...we got Fa$e in'da crowd, he putt'n on fa da State of Missouri. (Crowd cheers and some people scream, 'Fa$e, we Love you Nigga!!!') He well-known in dis Real Nigga shit, an'he one-na da nominees tonight for The Realist Nigga of da year! Whaddup Fa$e? (Mr. Fa$e nods his head in acknowledgment.)

Ta'night... we gonna acknowledge some of da'illest Niggas in da game. Like ya boy Kim Jung Un ova in North Korea. (Crowd cheers and boos!) Now dis Nigga know he a Nigga, starvin'da whole country, jus'so he can build some bombs an'shoot'em up into da air! Now if dat ain't some Nigga shit! Starvin'yo entire county jus'so you can play'wit the world's most expensive firecarackers!!!

An'we can't fa'get about dis Nigga Vladimir Putin. (Crowd once again cheers and boos.) Dis Nigga done went so crazy, he kill'n all da Ukrainians, jus'so he can control some frozen land! Dis Nigga done went ta'war ova frozen dirt, now dis Nigga crazy! #WTFRichWhiteNigga #WhatMoYouNeedNigga!!!

Who else we got? Oh yeah, my Nigga R. Kelly! Dis Nigga was out here chasin' kids down, tryna make love to'em! Da Nigga out here'fuck'n wit lil boys n' girls, writ'n all dese good ass love songs! Now come to find out...dey all about kids! Dis Nigga wil'n out! #NotDaKidsNiggas

Dis year at the Nigga Ball we gon'be payin' special tribute to The Realist Nigga ta Eva live. We are also givin'out the awards for The Realist Nigga of the Century; The Realist Nigga of da Decade; and last but not least da Realest Nigga of da Year!

As always, we wanna thank all y'all Niggas fa'puttin on fo yo block, yo hood, yo city, yo state...shit, even yo country! We know how hard it done got fa'da Real Nigga to do dey thang, so much respect to all the Real Niggas who doin' what dey gotta go! First up is the finalist for dis'year's Realist Nigga of the Century: Adolf Hitler and Harry S. Truman (crowd cheers and boos) ...

*Maserati opens the envelope...*

"I know...I know...the award for Realist Nigga of the Century goes to... (Drum roll) Adolf Hitler!!! Yeah, dat Nigga proved to be one of the most ignanste Niggas to ever walk this earth! Dis Nigga not only succeeded in taking over the Nazi Party in 1921; in addition to dis, dis Nigga spent eight months in prison writing his manifesto titled, 'Mein Kampf.' Hitler was solely responsible for the genocide of an estimated six million innocent Jews. During World War II, Hitler set up concentration camps, in which he sent Jewish Women, Men, and children to concentration camps, where they were forced into labor and then, most were murdered. Yeah...dis'a Real Nigga of epic proportion! Now y'all know dis Nigga dead, so we gotta accept this award on dis Niggas behalf.

Next up is the award for Nigga of the Decade. The nominees for this award are Donald Trump...Barack Obama...R. Kelly and Elizabeth Holmes. (Crowd cheers and boos)

*Maserati opens the envelope...*

This year's winner of the Realist Nigga of the Decade award goes to... (Drum roll) Ya boy...Donald Trump!!! (Crowd cheers uncontrollably!!!) Donald Trump couldn't make it tonight, so on behalf of dat Nigga, I'ma accept dis award. Y'all know dat Nigga is still tryna convince his Niggas he won da election in 2020; just like a Nigga to live in a fairytale world!

Next up we wanna pay tribute to The Realist Nigga ta'eva live. All y'all know none of us would be here today it is wasn'fo dis Nigga! He da one gave us some of da greatest Nigga shit ta ever been done! I mean, dis was da first Nigga ta get kicked outta heaven! Dis is the first Nigga ta convince us ta eat dat fruit in da garden! Dis Nigga got us kicked out da'garden! Dis is da only Nigga bold enough to go up against Jesus...Da Nigga tried ta get Jesus ta jump off'da mountain y'all!

Tell me dis Nigga ain't da realist in da business! If it wasn'fa dis Nigga doing his thang, wouldn'a been no slavery; no threesomes; no genocides, no wars; no rich Nigga po-Nigga; no hoe's, no pimps; no caste systems, no presidents, no politicians! Dis Nigga da reason a Nigga wit da word Baby in his rap name can still make millions and go platinum! Hell...dis Nigga da reason we got rap in the first place, and rock n' roll, and all dat good shit dat make a Nigga wanna sip syrup, snort cocaine, go kill a Nigga, and den fuck all night!

Man, y'all betta get up on y'all feet...naw, stand up on yo tippy toes and give a big dumb, ignant, Nigga round of applause fa da Realist Nigga ta'eva live...my Nigga...yo Nigga...every's Nigga favorite Nigga...Da one and only...Satan!!! (Crowd hooting and hollering! Clapping and yelling!!! Banging on tables and actin'a ass!!! You know how Niggas roll!!!) Now y'all know dis Nigga Satan couldn't make it ta'night. He down in hell...keepin'dat shit flamin' hot like he does!!! But we Love dat'Nigga!

Dat Nigga Satan made it possible for us'ta celebrate our next nominees fa' Realist Nigga of da Year! (Crowd cheers!!!) These nominees have been out he'puttin in top-notch work fa'dis Nigga shit! So, without furtha'ado, let's introduce the nominees! Dis year nominees fa'da Realist Nigga of da Year are: Vladimir

Putin (crowd cheers and boos!)...next up, ya girl Suki wit'da good cat (crowd screams and cheers!!!)...next up, dis Nigga done went Bitcoin scam crazy, its'ya boy Sam Bankman (crowd screams and boos; someone screams out, 'I los'my money fuckin'wit dat Nigga!!!'...and the last Nigga, but nowhere near the least Nigga, you know him and love him! Hell...I know'em personally and Love dis Niggas dirty drawers! Dis Nigga is an O.G wit dis Real Nigga shit, give it up for my Nigga reppin' Missouri...da Realist Nigga Fa$e!!! (Crowds erupts with cheers!!!)

Yeah...yeah...yeah...we got some hittas dis year'wit dis Real Nigga shit! But you know there can only be one Real Nigga of da Year... (Maserati opens the envelope, and her face frowns). Dis year's winner of The Realist Nigga of da Year goes to Sam Bankman! (Crowd boos and yells profanities!) All types of remarks could be heard from the audience. *Who da fuck is dis White ass Nigga! Fuck naw...dat weak ass shit! Dese Niggas lame ass fuck dawg, dain'gon keep playin my Nigga like dis! How did dat Nigga beat out Fa$e?!?!*

Yet as I gaze over in Mr. Fa$e's direction, he and his entourage seem unfazed by the announcement. He and his crew arose and clapped for the winner. I thought to myself, *'Why isn't he upset...after all, everyone in attendance thinks he should've won?'*

"Ya'boy Sam couldn't make it to accept dis award. Dat Nigga somewhere wait'n to be extradited. We gon'accept dis award on his behalf and keep dis shit movin'."

I notice Mr. Fa$e and his crew arise from their seats and make their way toward the exit. As they exit the building, I quickly follow behind them. Unaware of my frantic pace, I slow down, as not to draw too much attention. As I walk out into the cool crisp night...

"Hey, Nigga...wha'da fuck you doin' follow'n us!"

I'm in shock, someone from Mr. Fa$e's crew has jacked me up and it now feels as if I'm on the verge of death!

"Hey Nigga...you betta say some fast, or you ain gone make it!"

"My name's Jimmy Fisher and I'm from Iowa. I'm writing a story about the underground world of pimping and while doing some research, I stumbled upon this Ball. I decided to come and see what it was about, and hopefully, do some interviews..." The guy cut me off!

"So, you da police?!?!"

"No, I'm Jimmy Fisher...I'm a freelance reporter. I'd like to interview Mr. Fa$e..." Mr. Fa$e turns around and gives me his card. He looks me up and down and simply says, "You wanna interview me? Here's where you can find me." He looks at his companion and, simply says, "Put'em down fo'you hurt'em."

And just like that, I escaped death! Shaken by my near-death experience, I unclench my hands! As I did, I noticed Mr. Fa$e's business card fell to the ground. As I picked up the card, I examined it...no name or address, just a number. 'I'm in.' I whisper to myself, yet I know if I call the number on this card, death may be the least of my worries. But this is what I must do to get the Truth!

# Chapter 2:
# Two Weeks Later…

### (12:47) p.m. An Interview with the Realist Nigga

"Where ya headed?" The taxi driver asked.

"55th and Brooklynn." I could tell by the look, which was directed towards me through the rearview mirror, that the place of my desire was a point of contention with my driver. "You might as well pay me now. You know that's a tough place to travel. Ain'sayin you gon get me, but them cats ova there…well, let's just say you'll need more than good luck."

I hand the driver the amount, and off we go. I discover myself…alone, in the back of a taxi, in search of The Realist Nigga. You see…two weeks ago I happened to find myself at the 51st Annual Nigga Ball. It was there that I witnessed firsthand the zeitgeist of Nigga(s). It was also there that something bothered me, a 21-year-old White kid from the small town of Keokuk, Iowa. Hitler…Donald Trump…and Sam Bankman…all white Men; all won awards for Realist Nigga of the Century, the Decade, and the Year…in that order.

It seems as though (to me at least), what it once meant to be a real Nigga' is no longer the standard. It is, for this reason, I discover myself…alone in the back of a taxi to meet 'Fa$e'. As the driver makes a right on 55th and Prospect, and onto 55th and Brooklynn, I'm apprehensive about my destination. I arrive on a street that seems to me…quaint. Quite different from what the taxi driver has prepared me for. Manicured lawns…nice houses…quiet suburbia. *This isn't where the Acclaimed Realist Nigga resides?* I whisper to myself as the taxi makes an abrupt stop.

"We're here." I hop out to a scene that is fascinating to my senses. I arrive at a house that is...nice (yellow paint, a beautiful display of flowers decorating the manicured yard, and at least $250,000.00 worth of cars in the driveway!) Yet I discover Mr. Fa$e, on the side of this house, sitting atop an old beat-up Monte Carlo, which is being held up by four cinder blocks! I approached cautiously this time around, as I recalled my fate from our past encounter.

I marvel at him for a moment. This six-foot-four tall, lanky figure. His skin is decorated with an assortment of tattoos, reaching from his waist, making their way to the peak of his Adam's apple. In addition to this, his dreads seem to go on forever. This is certainly the picture I conjure up when I envision the Realist Nigga!

"Hello, Mr. Fa$e...it's a pleasure to finally sit down and talk with you in person."

"Whassup..." He replies with a simple acknowledgment and a head nod. He spoke with what could only be described as a deep, slow, almost melodic tone. I'm cautious as I approach, I notice the look in the eyes of the other two gentlemen who are with Mr. Fa$e. Although they look much younger, they give off the energy...what I could only describe as a 'Fuck it!!!' mentality!

"I had the opportunity to see you at the 51st Annual Nigga Ball. I'd like to ask you your thoughts on the outcome of that evening?" Mr. Fa$e replies once again, "Whassup..." Yet he doesn't seem worried about my approaching him and his associates. So, with that sense of ease, I continue my approach.

"What do you think about the selections and the people that won that night?" I'm hesitant to speak any further because the next question could make or break my entire interview. "Before we go any further....is it okay if I use the 'N-word for this interview?" Mr. Fa$e looks at me with a smirk on his face, as if he was half-amused and half-already irritated, and mumbled a word under his breath, 'Niggaroid'.

"What did you say?"

"Hey Man… let's be real, dis won't be the first time you said Nigga or Nigger, so don't try to bullshit me or yourself. You want da real, you gotta be willing to be real with ya'self." I blush at Mr. Fa$e's words…he's right. I've always said the "N" word when listening to rap music, especially when riding in the comfort of my car, or the safety of my home. Before I get too distracted, I continue with my train-of-thought. "Hitler winning Realist Nigga of the Century; Sam Bankman winning Realist Nigga of the Year; Satan getting the Realist Nigga to Eva to do it; and Donald Trump winning Realist Nigga of the Decade. How does that sit with you?"

Mr. Fa$e throws his hands into the sky as if he's throwing up rolls of money into the clouds. "Uh…Oh Man, you gotta keep it playa. You can't take nothing from dem guys…if dat's who won, you gotta respect da outcome."

"So…what do you think about what it means to be a Real Nigga in this day and age?"

"You know…us Real Niggas don't put no pressure on dat word. It's as easy as saying hello. We know what it means, it's up to dem suckas to figure out what it means. You got a couple of suckas and squares who take dat shit outta context."

"So, I guess what I'm asking is…do people like Hitler, Bankman, and Trump deserve to be awarded any title of Realist Nigga; considering their race, age, and upbringing?"

"Dat word has nothing to do with any of that. Dat word is probably like (how can I say dis so you can understand) …Dat word is like being in a gang, with different chapters. It's a worldwide gang. Every chapter rotates how dey chooses. So, you gotta respect what da people want."

"So…you're saying it's about what you represent, not who you are?"

"Exactly."

"Just so the reader can better understand...give me a few examples of who are the some of the realist Niggas in the game right now."

"Dat's easy.... there were a lot of people at that ball. Some won and some lost. People know who da Realist Nigga is...for instance, out of everyone at that ball, you chose to talk to me. Why is dat? You know who da Realist Nigga is..."

"I know what some people seem to think. They booed when Bankman won Realist Nigga of the Year, yet they cheered every time your name was mentioned. What is it that you do that makes people perceive you as the Realist Nigga?"

"Dis right here...for instance he won, you know, ain'hatin dat...da man won and I'm cool wit'dat. Ain' wishin' death on him or hatin' on him. I'm in contact wit dat Nigga Bankman now...da Realist Nigga hit me up on my phone and wanted to talk to me."

"Let me ask you this Mr. Fa$e...What is it about the environment that made you into the Realist Nigga?" (Mr. Fa$e has chosen to do this interview in what could only be considered 'the hood'. We're sitting atop an old rusty Monte Carlo Luxury Sport. Mr. Fa$e and his companions seem as if they're in their element.)

"Dis is what everybody knows...dis da fifty's! Dis Out South...we were known for producin' Men! Real Men..."

"So, what is it that separates or makes a Nigga and a Real Man? I mean...can a real Nigga be a real Man and vice versa?"

"A real Woman can be a real Nigga!!! It's about how you carry yo'self. It's about handlin' yo business, how'eva you seen fit, and when da consequences come, you stand on yo shit! You don't take anybody down with you. Even when it comes to family.... real Niggas provide and protect no matter what; even when we feel it's not appreciated! Cause dat's what we do. But let's make it clear...fuckn'wit a real Nigga, we gon get respect in whateva we do...regardless. But fuckin wit a

Nigga...you ass out, you see, there's a big difference between a Nigga and a real Nigga..."

(My jaw drops...all this time I thought that a Nigga and a real Nigga were one in the same.) "Mr. Fa$e...you're telling me that there's a difference between a Nigga and a real Nigga?"

Mr. Fa$e leans down and places his elbows on his knees. He continues to look off into the distance as if he's drawing his thoughts from the rays of the Sun. "Let's make this simple.... like take a dog for instance...you got yo thousand dolla poodles dat you keep in da house, and den you got yo mutt who you let outside all day run'n da streets. We're all dogs, just different degrees...and you can see the difference immediately."

Confused...I reply once again, "So a nigga is a poodle and a real Nigga's a mutt?!?!?"

Mr. Fa$e turns towards me and...as if to stop himself from slapping me, he clenches his hands into a fist and drops his head. His dreads, stretching down to his waist...seem as if they too are shaking in anger! He replies, "Naw...what are you doin' Man?"

"I'm just trying to understand what it is you just conveyed to me. You said that a nigga is a poodle and a real nigga is a mutt." I stumble to retrieve my notes...sweat now beginning to run from my skull, dampening my golden-blonde hair and making its way down above my brow. My insides scream to me as I rummage through my papers! *Please don't get us killed out here.*

"Hey...Jimmy. I never told you dat...you have ever seen a thousand dolla mutts? Now you fuckin with me...yo fuckin wit me! Shit like dis...muthafuckas like you at dat ball da reason dat real niggas summons a nigga."

Confused once again, I repeat, "Summons."

"Yah...like call dat nigga up out of'em! Like dis interview goin' wrong.... cus now you fuckin wit me part'na..." Instantly I see, out of the corner of my eye, Mr. Fa$e's associates inching ever so close to me as if they're awaiting the command to attack! (I go back up to my notes to make sure I didn't misunderstand Mr. Fa$e...I can tell by his agitation, as well as his crew, that this may go wrong real fast!) My voice shaking, "So according to my notes ..." Mr. Fa$e cuts me off.

"A thousand dolla poodle is like da real nigga. I might'a misspoke, so I apologize. Matter fact, I ain't used to talki'n to yo kind, matter fact where you from?

Relieved at the easing of the tension, I replied, "Me...I'm from Iowa. Keokuk, Iowa. I was born and raised there...went to Iowa State University and received my degree in journalism. I stumbled upon the Nigga Ball when I was researching a story I was working on for Pimping. So, I got a plane ticket and bought a ticket to the Ball, and here I am..."

Mr. Fa$e looked me up and down, and let out a little smile, "Oh...stumbled upon...I get it now. I understand. So, we like an experiment to you now huh, we are interested in you?"

(I try immediately to change the subject, seeing a this is new territory for me and I don't want to irritate Mr. Fa$e) "So Mr. Fa$e...I see you have a lot of tattoos...any reason in particular for so many?"

Mr. Fa$e hops off the old, broken down Monte Carlo, "I'ma show you... let's ride...welcome to da hood!"

I'm hesitant to go on a ride'; however, Mr. Fa$ looks at me as if I have no choice. As I go to get in the passenger seat "Aye Nigga...you ain't ben putt'n in no work ta sit up front! You betta get'cho bitch ass in the backseat!" One of Mr. Fa$e's associates pushes me into the backseat. I dropped my recorder, notebook, and pen! Something inside tells me this is gonna be a long day...

# Chapter 3:
# Ride-A-Long With Da Realist Nigga

### (2:00 p.m.) Ride-A-Long With Da Realist Nigga

Mr. Fa$e cranks up the 84 Box Chevy ('factory clean' as Fa$e would say) blaring' I'm a God n' da hood, by Jeezy. He looks back at me, as I try my best to get comfortable and he smiles and says, "Da homie was just playin' wit you. See da lil Niggas have dey own special way of sayin' hello. But yeah...ya nuts gone drop taday." Mr. Fa$e pulls off...

"Where are we goin' Mr. Fa$e?" (I ask with a bit of uncertainty in my voice.)

Looking straight ahead he simply replies, "To'da land where broke Niggas don't go to. I wan'chu to look around...Jimmy from Keokuk, Iowa, and tell me what you see." As I observe the scenery, I see boarded-up buildings...too many to count! A church on almost every corner we pass and just as many liquor stores. Cracks in the sidewalks, so many it looks like spider-webbed concrete; cracks and potholes in the streets; cracks in the buildings. It seems as if everything is crumbling away under neglect.

I also notice women and men jostling with each other (I hope they're just playing around.) Kids playing in the streets with the water from a fire hydrant. All this seems strange to me because it's 2:16 in the afternoon. This is a time when everyone should either be at work or school (at least that's how it is where I'm from.) I also witnessed a look on the faces of all the people...it's a look that I can't describe, for I have never seen this look before...As I'm explaining this to Mr. Fa$e he interjects...

"It's fucked up huh...check dis out, I know you don't know what you look'n at. What you think you look'n at, hold that thought...dis is da land of Black Excellence. You wouldn't believe how many thousands of dollars are laying up in'dem houses...how full dem refrigerators are. Da same reason dese people love dis shit and don't wanna leave here is da same reason you came here..." Mr. Fa$e smiles to himself as if just speaking about his community warms his heart.

"But what is the look on their faces?" (I ask again, perplexed by that sense of hunger in their eyes.)

Mr. Fa$e looks at me through the rearview mirror, "Wanna ask one of 'em?" Yet it wasn't a question... (Mr. Fa$e brings the 84' box Chevy to an abrupt stop! He calls over one of the citizens...)

"Hey Ms. Lady...come'here let me holla at'cha'fo a minute..."

The Woman approaches with a walk that says *I run these muthafuckin streets and everything in them!* As she arrives at the car, she leans down and sticks her head in the window. Looking at the four gentlemen in the car she rolls her eyes and speaks, "Whassup baby...ain into no freaky shit so own'know why you'll holla. But I do got dese fat ass dime sacks." (She pulls out a few sacks of what appears to be marijuana, sealed in plastic baggies; displaying them to her potential customers.)

Mr. Fa$e seems to be irritated by her approach and replies, "Watch yo'muthafuckin mouf...yo Man probably owe me fo'dat!!!" The woman looks up at Mr. Fa$e and sees that look (it's the same look that I'm curious about, once again on display.) "Fuck her let's go!"

Mr. Fa$e speeds off, and as he does one of the sacks fall into the car. Mr. Fa$e picks it up and throws it out the window. We ride in silence for a while, until Mr. Fa$e slows down at a fast food restaurant. He calls over a few teenagers who seem to be loitering in the parking lot. As they approach Mr. Fa$e says, "Maybe they'll have the answer you want.

Whassup wit ya'll out here? Why ya'll think dis white boy in my backseat?"

The teenage boy wearing designer clothing from head to toe, walking with a mannerism that says *I own dis muthafuckin worldn' er'than in it!* eyed me up and down, looked at Mr. Fa$e, then looked back at me and replied, "Shit, dat nigga probably look'n fa'some work. Yo gone serve'em, cause if not I got dat good shit!"

Everyone smiles....even me.

Mr. Fa$e responds, "Naw he curious about dis Nigga shit. He wanna unda'stand why we are da'way we are."

The teenage boy and girl both look at me with a look of pity and bemusement...The teenage girl, dressed as if she's the CEO of her life, with the mannerisms of a boss, guiding her Destiny, simply asks, "What'chu wanna know?"

"Well...uh..." Before I can get out another word...

"Hey Man... hurry da fuck up, time is money and you ain't spend'n no money, so you wast'n ou'time!" The teenage boy is now no longer amused. His mind, savors every moment of life, as if his time is numbered!

Mr. Fa$e whispers, "Would you believe that if I told them to snatch yo'white ass up and kill you, dey would without hesitation?" Both teenagers smile.

"I just wanna know what it is that makes you all love this environment?"

The teenage girl smiles, "Shit...dis is da life! We'own work fo'nobody...can ball out every day and night...and do what da fuck we want! We ain't got nobody telli'n us what to do and when to do it. We have been doin'dis evr'sine we were born! Shit nigga...dis is da Life!!! Ain't no otha life! Fuck you mean..." As she finished speaking, she looked over at the teenage boy and slapped his hand in some fashion that was foreign to me.

He hugged her, brought her in close to him, and yelled! "On my soul!!! Let'dat Nigga know Babygirl!" Together they walked away from the car, embracing each other and rapping a song aloud.

Mr. Fa$e cranked the car back up and pulled off. "Let's get da fuck up outta here. You offended dem...do you understand why?" Perplexed...I asked, "How...why did I offend them?"

As Mr. Fa$e swerves the Chevy, he once again looks into the rearview mirror and says, "Cause you don't ask Real Niggas why dey live da way dey live. Like dis way of life ain't human or some...you think dis shit ain't human. We da reason you down here risk'n yo life"

"So, you're saying that this life was already your destiny?"

"What does that mean...I don't even know what da fuck dat means."

"Like...you were meant for this life. Born into it. Like a Fortune 500 company owner grooms his children to take over the company. You're saying you all were groomed to take over this lifestyle."

"It's in my blood...so if dat's what dat mean...I guess so."

Now I think I'm starting to get it...At least I think I am, "Have you ever worked a 9 to 5?"

"I always wanted to, but it's instilled in us, from my old man, *never work for no other Man*. See, my Grandfather was a real street millionaire. So, I grew up watch'n him do it and he gave me dis advice, why would I not take it and run wit it? Being a Real Nigga is all about action...no talk'n. We just as religious as da monks when it comes to dis street shit."

As if I've gotten a second burst of intellectual energy, I reply, "So there's corporate Niggas, street Niggas, rich Niggas and poor

18

Niggas...basically what you're saying is a Nigga is a pedigree, not a word."

"Yea...each class of Nigga has its position...we play different positions...we got da same morals and values, just on different levels. Poor Niggas don't say dey poor. Poor Niggas livin da best dey can, on dey level. Poor Niggas don't even know dey poor...dey only know dat because ya'll say it. I think po'Niggas got it da'best cause dey don't complain. Live life without complian'n and exlain'n makes us a real Nigga! Havin' money doesn't make you a Real Nigga."

Now I'm starting to grasp the concept..." So a nigga is a concept...a mindset...a way of life that only the Man or Woman living that life can fully understand."

Mr. Fa$e removes his hand from the steering wheel and rubs his nappy beard. "Yeah...it's like a...what'chu call an intelligent ignorance." Mr. Fa$e once again looks into the rearview mirror, "You understand what that means? Intelligence Ignorance..."

"No...I don't."

"What time it...the night is still young. By the end of the night, you'll understand the difference. You got 24 hours...so by the crack of dawn, you'll get it." He smiles again, "So your interview has just turned into your experience. Like Vegas, what happens in Brooklynn stays in Brooklyn. You B-Rad now..."

Confused by Mr. Fa$e's words, I reply, "Mr. Fa$e it's 6:30 at night...I thought I'd be outta here by 8:00. I've gotta plane tomorrow morning."

"Well...you gone be late. Cause roun'here we didn't start our day until all the kids is outta school, and the parents are off work...we call it after 5...outta respect fa'da citizens.

# Chapter 4:
# Nocturnal Niggas

## (8:37 p.m.) Nocturnal Niggas

As we pull onto 55th and Paseo, we make our way into the parking lot of a liquor store. The sign reads, 'Paul's Liquor.' Outside the liquor store, there's an assortment of characters, 'The geezers' as Mr. Fa$e refers to them. He says they're a staple in this community. After listening to Mr. Fa$e explain the importance of them; they are what could only be described as the cleaner fish of the hood. The people who keep this whole operation running smoothly. "Dey da ones who keep dis system operating, if not for them, there's no us. So, you gotta give'dem they respect."

As Mr. Fa$e hops out of the car and is greeted by all (geezers, Women dressed in sexy apparel, Men with their hats cocked sideways. Etc.) Seems as if this is the place to be this time of night. Reluctant to expose myself, I yell to Mr. Fa$e, "Hey could you get me orange juice?"

Hearing me...he looks back, "You a funny guy. Get'cho own juice. Fuck you think this is." Once again, he gives me a laugh or a slight chuckle. In a way it's sinister, but it fits Mr. Fa$e perfectly. As I get out of the car, I too am greeted by the onlookers. *Whaddup my Nigga? Oh shit...we got us'some White chocolate in'da hood ta'night! You want me ta'suck yo dick White Boy...ain't gone be nuthin' but a hundolarondo?* (What I came to learn was a hundred dollars.)

While in the store, I grabbed orange juice. Mr. Fa$e and his associates grab an assortment of items; Lipton Iced tea, pork rinds, Remy, Hennessey, now n'laters, and a bag of plastic baggies. As I pay for my juice, the guy behind the counter looks at me...with the same look as everyone else I've encountered today. Strange though, because he's an Arab-looking guy. After paying for my orange juice I beeline back to the car, and into the backseat. One of Mr. Fa$e's associates, whom I now know is known as 'D-Money' breaks open a box of 'backwoods' and begins to fill it with…OMG!!! As he licks the edges and seals it, he looks at me and smiles…

Mr. Fa$e…finally reversing out of the parking lot, looks into the backseat and smiles…this moment, the mood could only be described as *I can feel it comin' in'da air tonight/Oh lawd/I've been wait'n for dis moment for all my life/Oh lawd…Oh, lawd*…I'm brought back into reality when D-Money passes me the burning 'back wood'; that's what they called it. "I don't smoke," I say with a smile.

Once again D-Money, ignoring me, nudges me and says, "You didn't smoke." Guess the emphasis on the past tense means I should hit this and let life happen. *The fuck…what have gotten me into!* My hands shaking, my palms sweating, I grab the back wood and inhale. In an instant my mind…my body and my life changed…hazy fog…music slowing down…lights getting dimmer and dimmer. "Let the games begin. Don't throw up in my shit." Mr. Fa$e says as he nods back at me…

Another one of Mr. Fa$e's associates hands me the bottle of Remy, "Hit dis shit Nigga. Dis da chasa." A styrofoam cup is placed in my hands and he pours some Lipton Peach Tea into my cup. Followed up by the pouring of the Remy. "You gon love'dis shit…On my Mama's Mama!" Mr. Fa$e turns the music up…and it seems as if everyone in the car is nodding their head, either uncontrollably or in rhythm with the beat.

In my cloudy haze, I catch glimpses of Mr. Fa$e smiling, laughing, once again with that sinister laugh. At this moment he seems to be the Serpent in the Garden, and me…well I'm just Adam, taking a bite of an apple. He continues to ask, "You cool B-Rad? Dis what'chu wanted huh?" His homies continue laughing at me, or just laughing at life…I don't know anymore…I'm stoned!

# Chapter 5:
## Am I still getting married?

### (12:16 a.m.) Am I still getting married?

*Wow...this is an amazing experience...I'm not going to lie. I couldn't have ever fathomed this day going anything like this.* As I lie back in the backseat of the Chevy, I feel like I'm on a cloud and the world is looking up at me. A few minutes later...I noticed the car had come to a stop, and we were back in Brooklyn. I'm familiar with the street, however, this isn't the same as I remember earlier, something's off. As we all get out of the car, my feet give way under me. I wobble under the pressure of being high, struggling to make it to the front porch! Yet as I arrive at the destination of my desire, it is where I take a seat on the steps. In the front yard are two dogs the size of Black bears! Ferocious-looking animals... too have that look on their faces...

"Hey Nigga...get the fuck up!!! We can't have no White Boy sitting on dis'porch in da middle of da'night." Slowly I make my way to the inside of the house and it is there that I collapse... "Mov'ova Nigga!" One of the guys pushed me. I scoot over and pass out...

"Where am I?" It's now 2:06 a.m. and I discover myself on the couch, surrounded by red...a sea of red! Everyone in the house is donning red from head to toe...even the ladies are red on red. Red headscarves...red shoes...even the dog sitting by the couch has a red bandana tied around his neck! Am I hallucinating?

"Come'on B-Rad, let's get'chu some air and food." Mr. Fa$e grabs hold of me and helps me outside to the back porch, where I discover there's a cookout going on...at two o'clock in the morning! Everyone seems not only awake...but happy and enjoying life. The backyard has about thirty dog kennels strategically placed along the fence. Mr. Fa$e hands me a plate, loaded with chicken and ribs.

"Hey, Mr.Fa$e...what is this place?" I ask as I take a gigantic bite of the rib *(Not going to lie...I'm hungry as ever! Wonder why...)*

"This is what we call 'the kennel.' We in'dat land I was talk'n about. Dis here is our Heaven. You see those dogs out there?" I nod my head as I continue to eat.

"It's like thirty thousand dollars' worth of dogs. What kind of dog you got?"

I lick my fingers and reply, "I don't have a dog, and my fiancé has a cat and a hamster."

"A fiancé huh?"

"Yeah...we've been together since middle school and we're planning on getting married this summer."

Mr. Fa$e stands up and taps me on my shoulder, "Let me show you some'in."

As we make our way back into the house, Mr. Fa$e leads me past the crowd of partygoers. I'm led into what seems like a cave, yet I know we're going down into the basement. It seems the further we go, the hotter, the sweatier, and the darker it gets. It is here...once we arrive at our destination, I'm greeted with soft hugs and erotic looks.

"Do you know what a prostitute is? You ever slept with a prostitute?" As Mr. Fa$e reclines back against the wall, one of the women surfaces from out of the crowd and begins dancing in front of him. Sliding up and down against him, as if he's a pole. Without hesitation, another Woman walks up to me and begins working the same moves on me. This is the first time in my entire life I've ever had anyone dance this close to me! I'm at a loss for words!

"No...Mr. Fa$e...I've only been with my fiancé." I reply, now sweaty from the closeness of my seducer.

"Lucky you...dis ain't no prostitute dough. Same effect. Lucky you. Dis is why guys with fiancé buy pussy." He laughs once again and walks away...As I attempt to follow behind him, the Woman holds me up. I mean literally...she unzips my khakis and begins pulling my semi-erect penis out in front of the entire room! *I'm getting married!* I whisper as I make a half-hearted attempt to stop her, yet the softness of her hand caressing my penis is too much to resist! I look around to see if anyone is watching, and it seems as if all the other Men are in the same position as I am. (Head up in the air, eyes half opened and mouth wide open!)

This Woman is swallowing my entire penis! I mean no exaggeration...my entire penis is being engulfed by this hot, moist voluptuous mouth that seems to understand all that I desire. *I'm soo fucking happy right now!!!* Even as her hand grabs my balls and caresses them. I stare into space and simply think to myself, 'I could do this forever!!!' As she slowly slides up to me, she looks me in the eyes and simply says, "Fuck me."

"I don't have a..." Before I could get the word out, she turned around, lifted her skirt, and slid my penis inside her! *Wow...even better!!!* I say to myself as I enter her warm, moist spot. Slowly...she rolls into me, back and forth, her rhythm impeccable! I grab onto her waist and grip her ass cheeks, pushing her deeper and harder into me! *Please take every inch of me!* I say in my mind. As if she read my mind, she swallowed my entire Penis inside her! What happened next was the most ama-z-ing exp-eri-ence e—ver! I held onto her tighter and tighter...until...I...came!!! As I looked down, attempting to seal this moment into my memory forever; she was gone.

*Where did she go? What just happened? OMG Am I still getting married?* So many questions ran through my mind as I pull my khakis up. I search the room for her, yet the darkness, as well as the crowd, makes my search impossible. Slowly I make my way back up to the light…It is there I discover everyone who I rode with today…enjoying life. D-Money tries to pass me another back wood…*Fuck it…I'm already in.*

As I take another puff of the back wood, I exhale and stare into the sky. As the smoke evaporates out of my lungs, through my lips, and into the darkness of the sky. It is here…in this moment…in Missouri…in the dusk of the night that I am… "Wha'sup?" Once again, I'm in the presence of Mr. Fa$e.

Sitting on the porch with a back wood burning, I look at Mr. Fa$e, "This night has been incredibly awesome! Yet…I know it isn't real. I just got a blowjob and had sex in a dark basement, in the middle of a crowd of onlookers!"

Mr. Fa$e didn't even flinch, "You knaw'das…you got yo'balls dropped. No brains, but chu'got balls. Dat'was some Niggas shit you did. Fuckin' a Man's baby mama, why he'upstais…now da'some Nigga shit!" Mr. Fa$e smiles as he looks at the shock that my face has gone into!

"I didn't know Mr. Fa$e!?!?! I swear I didn't know!!!"

Mr. Fa$e smiles, "Well…you know dey say you learn from yo'mistakes. Swea'da God…we hope you don't learn from dis one."

"Why not?"

"Her baby daddy's name is 'Homo' man."

"As in homosexual…" He just looks at me.

"As in Homicide." Once again, I stare off into the sky. Searching for something…anything that brings me comfort. It seems as if I were lost for eternity. Thoughts of me smoking marijuana for the first time. Drinking Remy and Lipton Iced Tea for the first time. Having a sexual encounter with someone other than my fiancé for the first time…and maybe even dying because the Woman I had sex with has a boyfriend named Homo, who was just a room away! As I replay the past few hours, a car pulls up and parks along the back fence.

Mr. Fa$e reaches under the steps and grabs a bag. He throws it on my lap, "Do me a favor...go'n'han her dis bag Man. Don't talk to her...don't stare at her...just hand her the bag."

I look down at the bag and reluctantly I do as he says. Awkwardly...I place the bag under my Polo khaki shirt. As it bulges out, I hold it in place with my arm, all the while speed walking to the car. As I approach the car, the passenger side window rolls down.

"Aye, nigga hurry'up! Ac'like dis shit legal a'some." Instantly I drop the bag inside the passenger side of the car, and Mr. Fa$e's words replay in my head. *Don't talk to her...don't stare at her...just hand her the bag.* Shit...I dropped the bag! I didn't hand it to her. Well at least it's in the car, and an instant, the car pulls off and into the darkness of the night.

"What was that?" I ask as I return to the comfort of the back porch.

"A bag."

"I know that, but what were its contents?"

Mr. Fa$e simply takes a hit of the back wood, inhales deeply, and replies, "Let's go, Man."

# Chapter 6:
## I still don't get it

**<u>(5:15 a.m.) I still don't get it.</u>**

Mr. Fa$e, myself, D-Money, and his other associate (whose name I still don't know); all get back into his car. As we pull off, there's a peaceful silence. Riding through Mr. Fa$e's neighborhood, I recall how just yesterday I arrived here unconscious to all that surrounds me. Now here I am...5:16 a.m. and I feel so alive! The smells...the people...the action ...the entire ambiance of the neighborhood has now begun to penetrate my being. It's as if I feel a part of this foreign land.

"I still don't get it, man...I had the experience of my life...yet I still don't get it"

Mr. Fa$e once again looks into the rearview mirror...rubs his beard, "It's' like bein' da'sidechick who wants to be da'wife. Da side chick wan'all da fruits and rewards of the wife; but don't wanna put in'da work of what it wakes ta'be a wife. He looks at me after saying that and simply says... "Sleep on it, get'chu some rest. But in 'da meantime it's da' a.m. and we do more roun'here before breakfast dan'mos do all day."

So, we head to an 'after-hour spot'. Mr. Fa$e and his associates are still enjoying the alcohol and backwoods. I however need sustenance. As we make a few turns, I notice the streets are teeming with life. It's as if no one sleeps...or even gets tired of that matter! As Mr. Fa$e's car comes to a stop, everyone exits. I'm now leaning up against Mr. Fa$e's car...

We arrive at a house, nothing special about it...just a light that flickers, hanging on the front porch. "Where are we?"

"Jimmy's"

"What's Jimmy's?"

"It's a place where we come to eat, buy liquor and all da'other shit we need ta'ge'us through'da night. Yu'know."

Mr. Fa$e and all his associates walked up to the front porch and knocked on the door. As the door opened, I could hear the laughter and commotion. An old Man greeted us, "Fa$e...whass'up playboy!" As he gives Mr. Fa$e and his associates a handshake, I walk through the door. It seems as if, for one moment all eyes are on me. *They're staring at me as if I'm the only White guy in the room?!?!? Oh...I Am!* I hold my head down and continue to follow in D-Money's footsteps...

Finally, I look up, I notice we arrive in a kitchen that is bustling with people and energy. There's a card game going on at a table; people standing around in one corner, yelling and jumping up and down, rolling dice; and an older lady is moving around the stoves, with an apron on. She looks at us and waves us over. She hugs D-Money and his other associate, "Ya'll be stayin' outta trouble?" Both gentlemen reply, "Yes ma'am."

She then looks over at Mr. Fa$e, "Fa$e...whass'up baby? Who you'got whi'cha?" Mr. Fa$e hugs the lady, "Uh...dis'here is Jimmy and he just try'na learn'n some bout us."

She looks me up and down, hugs me, and smiles, "You okay, they been treating you right?" I simply replied, "Yes."

"Yes, what?" She says with a stare that says, *Nigga you better give me my respect!* I look over at Mr. Fa$e and his associates, looking for a clue as to what to say, and it hits me, "Yes Ma'am, they've been treating me well."

"You hungry?"

"Yes ma'am."

"Well...give me a few minutes and Gramma went have you some food ta'put on dat stomach."

"Gramma...we ain'got a lotta time. Ole Jimmy here ride should be here'n any minute. Give'em some a'dat good stuff righ'dere." I look over at the jars that Mr. Fa$e is pointing to, and it looks to be...hell, I don't even know! They're just floating in a jar!!! Gramma looks at him and says, "Get a couple'la dese pickled pig feet out dis ja'. Matta' fact take a couple' dese pickled eggs too."

Gramma opens one of the jars, sticks her hand in and retrieves a big, pinkinsh, rubbery-looking item out of the jar. It has the shape of what appears to be a foot of some sort. She grabs another, places them in a bag, and takes a few items out of another jar and places them in a bag as well. As she hands me the bag, Mr. Fa$e hands her some money and we head out of the house. Once again, I discover myself leaning up against Mr. Fa$e, with a bag of...something. Mr. Fa$e looks at me, "Eat dat'shit! You'gone need'ta put some on'yo stomach."

Reluctantly I open the bag and the pungent smell hits me!!! It has a sour, odiferous smell to it! As I reach and grab the pink (what looks to be the shape of a foot); it slips out of my hand and back into the bag. This experience is enough to turn my face! As I try to eat it, I gag on the flesh!!! I end up throwing up! Heaving everything, including the alcohol onto the concrete. Mr. Fa$e and his associates laugh at me.

"Man...gimme dat'shit!" D-Money motions for me to hand him the sack...and I happily oblige! D-Money opens the sack, takes a pickled pig foot out of the bag and bites down into it...I mean he scarfs that stuff down! His other associate grabs the bag and swallows the pickled egg. I look over at Mr. Fa$e, "What can I say, acquired taste." Mr. Fa$e, for the first time laughs. I laugh as well...finally a moment of...laughter! Sitting there, I'm reminded of what it means to be...Human.

An unknown car pulls up, "Who called for a ride?" Mr. Fa$e looks at me, "It's ova B-Rad...the experience is ova'. Did you get'cho answer? It's amazing what one question will ge'chu. You rememba' yo'question you asked me about dese tattoos? Did'chu ge'cho answer?"

"About the tattoos? I don't know...I need to process this. Hey, why do they call you Mr. Fa$e?"

"No one calls me Mr. Fa$e except you. And you did that'cause you wan'te too. Das'what bein'a Real Nigga is'bout. Doin'what'cha wan."

I just looked at Fa$e, my journey coming to an end. As I walked towards the taxi, I felt...tired, yet energetic...sleepy, yet woke...unresponsive, yet sympathetic; and although it sounds like a contradiction...I feel GREAT!

Finally, in the backseat, I rest my head on the seat and begin processing what the last twenty-four hours have taught me. "Man...you gotta pay me before we pull off." As I reach into my pocket to gather my wallet...*Oh shit! My wallet's gone!* I yell out the window, "Hey...Fa$e. I seem to have misplaced my wallet. Could you please let me borrow some money and I'll send it back to your cash app."

He laughs," It ain't a misplacement Man...we know where you live. We'll send it to'ya. Ride's on us. I'm almos'sure we'll see'ya later." D-Money runs up to the car and hands me a bundle of dirty rolled-up cash. He looks at me with a smile. Wow...

# Chapter 7:
# Black don't crack!

"Where to?" My driver asks as I position myself in the back of her red Toyota Corolla. She looks to be a young African-American Woman, probably in her late twenties, or early thirties; with gold hoop earrings hanging effortlessly from her ears. Her hair puffed out into a curly afro, but perfectly sitting atop her head, as if it were a crown that has dawned her head from birth. She looked so comfortable in her skin...her body...if she was positive that all she possessed was made just for her. And a smile that could set the world on fire! 'Yeah...' I say to myself, ' I'm gonna enjoy this ride.'

"Downtown Atlanta...Peachtree Street. I'm here to meet a friend. Do I have to pay now or when we arrive?" I'm conscious of all my encounters now. I make the extra effort to answer questions before they ever arise. "Oh, no honey...I'm not worried about you bailing out on me. Even if you do, karma gone hit you up." She looks in the rearview mirror, smiles, and pulls off.

As we exit the airport and head into the city, I attempt to make small talk. "So how long have you been in this area?" "Oh...all my life. This is my city and I Love this place! I've been all around the world, you know with my time in the military. Yet I always seem to come back home. Yeah...this place has a hold on my heart."

"How long were you in the military?" I ask, now interested in her life. "Close to twenty years." "Twenty years!?!?! You know when I first got into the car, I thought you were in your early twenties, maybe early

33

thirties." With a smile, she simply said, 'You know what they say, baby boy, 'Black don't crack!' I smile...

"So, who are you headed to see?"

"There's a guy in Downtown Atlanta that claims to be the leading expert in understanding what it truly means to be an (I hesitate for a moment) ...'N'; you know what word I'm referring to. He claims to be a... (I have to choose my words carefully. I'm no longer with Fa$e and his associates) psychologist of sorts."

She looks ahead, eyes on the road, and says, "Is he white or Black?"

"According to his website, he's a seventy-three-year-old white man."

"And he knows what's it like to be a Nigga! He may know what it's like to be a Nigger, but I doubt he understands what's it like to be a Nigga. Shit....with the way things are changing out here in'da A, I don't even know what a Nigga is anymore! You probably be better off asking one'a these white kids. Hell, they'll know more than a seventy-three-year-old White Man!" I chuckle...yet her voice has a sincerity in it that resonates with me. "Why would the white kids know better?"

She once again looks into her rearview mirror, "Nowadays...everyone wants to do or say the most ignante'd shit, just so they'll get a 'like', or so that someone will follow them. Add to that the fact that Facebook, Instagram, Tik Tok and all these other sites cater to...let's just say, a certain type of look (she looks at me and smiles.) You can see why being a Nigga no longer has a negative connotation or stigma to it, and that's why Niggas are a part of everyday life. You'll know what to look for if you truly understand what and who Niggas are."

"I only wish I could truly grasp the idea that easy. Most times I discover myself lost in theories and hypotheses."

She looked up at me once again, "That's the problem, you looking for a Nigga like they in Petri dishes or some shit. You gotta live life to know it. How can I explain this to you...I could never truly explain to you what it's like to go to war in Iraq or protect oil fields in Saudi Arabia. Yet those experiences changed me in subtle ways that no one could ever understand. You got to have a perpetual bombardment of Nigga experiences, to the point that it penetrates your being and permeates your heart and mind. Now ain't no professor gone give you that. Hell...his ole'ass probably ain't never stepped foot in a ghetto. But you'll soon find out, 'cause we here, that'll be $48.32."

I hand her a fifty-dollar bill and politely smile, "I don't have my running shoes on, have a nice day." As I exit, she speeds off into traffic. I look at the building. It looks dry and professional. *Here I am, Jimmy Fisher, from Keokuk, Iowa; arriving in Downtown Atlanta to meet Dr. Jameston Du'mas; a Niggaologist.* I'm reminded of my time here weeks earlier. It was here, at the 51st Annual Nigga Ball that I got my introduction to what it means to be a Real Nigga (or at least that's what I thought.)

I wonder if Dr. Du'mas was in attendance that night, seeing as though, according to his website, he's the leading voice when it comes to understanding the mindset of the Nigga. As he stated on his website, "There's a certain amount of Niggatry one must understand to fully grasp the 'why' behind the actions (or inactions) of the Nigga species."

I stumbled upon his website while researching the word Nigga. After hours upon hours of searching the web, a page came up of a guy who claimed to be a Niggaologist!' I couldn't believe it either. Yet his website pulled me in when he spoke of salacious tales of his experience with 'the Nigga.' It was as if he went on a safari, and captured the Nigga in their natural habitat. As if a Nigga wasn't a human being, but instead a commodity!

Even while speaking with Dr. Du'mas over the phone, he sounded so confident...even worse, believable! Either this guy was the biggest bull-shitter I'd ever met, or he was really onto something. There was only one way to find out. "Good afternoon. I'm here to see Dr. Jameston Du'mas." After a few soft words over the phone, the secretary politely nodded over to a door. As I walked up to the door, I took a deep breath, 'Here goes nothing...'

# Chapter 8:
# Goddamn White folks done out Niggaed the Niggas!

**(4:27 p.m.) Goddamn White folks done out Niggaed the Niggas!**

His office was decorated with the prestige of a Presidential office. Certificates hung neatly on the wall. Books upon books decorate the walls, from floor to ceiling. The man even had a bear rug strategically placed in the middle of the floor! In addition to that, there lies a huge desk, littered with photos of him and 'important people' and...you guessed it...more certificates. "I'll take water, please. Thank you."

He gives me a look, "So Jimmy Fisher. Are you interested in becoming a Niggaologist, or are you just interested in understanding the inner workings of the Nigga? You know...there aren't many of us in this profession. Niggaologist I mean..."

"No... I'm simply enamored with the world/lifestyle of a Nigga. So, I've been researching, trying to better understand what it all means."

Dr. Du'mas grabs one of his crystal glasses from the tray, and pours himself a nice-sized shot of whiskey, "Well to truly understand the Nigga, you have to go into the Niggatry of it all."

"Niggatry of it all? What does that mean?" He smiles as if he's pulled me in. He takes a sniff of his glass and proceeds, "Niggatry is a word I coined one night when I tried to ascertain the stuff that makes up a Nigga. After years and years of studying, it came to me while reading a book titled: The Nigger Question by a dear Man, Thomas Carlyle. There's not just one thing that makes up a Nigga! Hence the word Niggatry! The term encompasses the infinitude of the breadth, height, length, and depth of ignorance, stagnation, and regression that all Niggas possess! The essence and/or elements of a Nigga."

He smiled as if he'd dropped the motherlode on me. "So Niggatry deals with the mental state of a Nigga; the consciousness, if you will?"

He pounds his fist against the wall! As if he's hit the jackpot! "Precisely Jimmy...and it is because of that mental state (that consciousness, or lack thereof) that Niggas are at the bottoms of every social, economic, and political sphere in our society!"

"So according to your definition, a Nigga can't be...say, an Elizabeth Holmes, Sam Bankman, Donald Trump, Hitler, or even Satan for that matter?"

Dr. Du'mas looked at me hesitantly, took a sip of his whiskey, and smiled, "That's a mighty fine theory you got there Jimmy. I'll have to allow that proposition a moment to cogitate throughout my mind. Speaking of which... have you ever thought about the Niggadome?" He smiles again as if he's on fire!

"Niggadome...what's that?" I reply with a look of confusion as if to feed into his ego.

Once again, he sniffs his glass, looks out the blinds, and replies, "I coined this word when...in 1960 I discovered myself amid my first encounter with African Americans. It was at this moment that I knew we were of a different species! Meaning we thought differently, yet I became more and more intrigued with their...well their everything! I told myself, in that very instant 'Jameston...your life's mission is to help the African-American race!' But how...how could I help when I didn't understand their plight? That's when it hit me!

I've got to get inside the Niggadome of my African-American people! And that's what Niggadome means: *The complete immersion of one's entire mind, i.e. thought process, into the way of life of being ignorant, hateful, oblivious to the needs of society, as well as your obligation to society.* The second definition, for those more challenged with understanding the first, is simpler and it is *the thought process that leads to a human being breathing, thinking, and living the life of a Nigga."* He looks at me as if he's giving a masterclass and I'm a neophyte, sitting on the floor, in awe of his lesson.

"So, being a Nigga, or being immersed in the world of a Nigga is only associated with being ignorant, hateful, or a neglect of the duties one owes to themselves, their families, and society? Have you ever encountered any good, law-abiding Niggas?"

Dr. Du'mas looked off into the distance as if he were recalling a long-forgotten memory, "There was this Woman I knew, back in 1966...we fell in love. I loved everything about her...her walk, her talk, the way she thought about life, right down to the way she stared at me. And she loved me...but it would never have worked. I was ashamed of what my family thought. She was an African-American you see, and I knew I couldn't control her. What if she..." His voice begins to trail off...*I'm losing him.*

I see Dr. Du'mas sinking into a dark place, and eager to extract as much as I can, I reel him back in, "Before we go any further...I'm pretty sure you've created a definition for the actual word Nigga. Seeing as though you've coined so many words."

*Got'em...*once again he smiles, reaches for his whiskey, and pours another shot.

Looking into his glass, he responds, "*A Nigga is a euphemism, derived from the actual term Nigger. The term Nigga was created and embraced by the descendants of African Slaves who sought to normalize and glamorize the ignorance that had been used against their ancestors. The term is used sometimes as a term of endearment by one ignorant person to another."*

I look down at my notes on purpose this time, as I already know what I'm about to say may excite him, and not in a good way! "Some of that I could agree with, yet it's the correlation that you continue to make between a Nigga and Black People as a whole, as well as ignorance that still puzzles me. Could you explain that a bit more for me...and the reader as well of course?"

This time he takes an enormous gulp of his whiskey, "Ahhhhhhhh...Jimmy, I see you aren't as bright as I thought. Follow me...Black people are some of the brightest, strongest, most intellectually aggressive people I've ever met. Why...it itches the shriveled-up rings around my asshole how one Ni-...Black Man can hop out of his bed and dunk a goddamn ball from half-court! It's ab-so-lutely fucking Amazing!!! To me, out of all that has happened to Black people as a race in America, here we are allowing our entire culture to be swept away on this speeding train of Niggaliciousness!!!

I mean...every Woman, white, yellow, black, brown, green, or purple; wants a big ass, thick lips, and tattoos from the top of their forehead to the tip of their toes. Now that's some Niggalicious shit!!! Look around you Jimmy...what are we as a society getting in return for this takeover of the Nigga? More wealth...more enlightenment...more peace...solving world hunger? No... No...and another no, instead you know what we get? Niggacide!!! Goddamn streets aren't safe worth a damn!!!" Dr. Du'mas throws his glass across the room, up against the nicely placed pictures on his wall, causing the frames to fall! He continues...

"These Niggas have managed to do the impossible! They even got the fucking Super Bowl halftime performances...all Nigga shit, even when White people perform...Nigga shit, fucking Justin Timberlake and Eminem! Every night you turn on the TV; murders, stores being vandalized, rapes, and robberies...Nigga shit...Nigga shit...Nigga shit!!! Worst of it all, we've all drunk the Nigga-Aide! Pretty soon the President of the United States will be displaying...Nigga shit!" As he leans up against the window, his eyes lost in a far out thought, there's silence for a moment.

"Are you aware of the 51st Annual Nigga Ball that was held here in Atlanta a few weeks back?" He nods his head, yes, still lost in some world outside the window. "Do you know who won Realist Nigga of the Year; Realist Nigga of the Decade; Realist Nigga of the Century; or even Realist Nigga ta Eva do it?"

He turns to look at me as if my next few words will determine his fate. I continue, "Sam Bankman, a white guy who stole billions of dollars in the FTX Bitcoin scam won Realist Nigga of the Year. Donald Trump, the 44th President of the United States won Realist Nigga of the Decade. Hitler...another white guy, and the leader of the Nazi Party won Realist Nigga of the Century. Last but not least, Satan won the Realest Nigga ta Eva do it. Now explain this to me, how is it that at a Nigga Ball that is dedicated to African-Americans, all white people, except for Satan, won those awards?"

While letting out this bit of information, I witnessed Dr. Du'mas's face go from spotty pale to fiery red! I'm talking Flamin' Hot Cheetos Red! I'm talking Strawberry Soda red!

He stood up in his chair and pounded his desk with both fists! "Everyone's gone Niggerish! Goddamn White folks have done out Niggaed the Niggas!" Exasperated, he slouched back down into his massive chair, "I'm too late Jimmy. We've been Niggaroided!!!" He picked up a copy of a book titled: The Nigger Question by Thomas Carlyle, and threw it to the ground! As the book hit the ground, something else caught my attention...

"You say we've been what?"

"We've been Niggaroided!"

He says a word that I'm familiar with. I smile...there's only one place he could've gotten that word from. I ask with a burst of excitement, "Excuse me...do you know Fa$e?"

He looks at me, sulking and slumped down in his chair, he replies, "Or course I know Fa$e. I got my Na.D (Niggaologist Degree) from Fa$e University." I hop out of my seat and stroll over to his wall of fame. There, proudly displayed on the wall, I noticed up to twenty certificates, all from Fa$e University! *You gotta be fucking kidding me!* In addition to the certificates, I notice pictures of Dr. Du'mas posing with Fa$e, smiling with the certificates in his hand!

"You mind if I ask how much it'll cost me to acquire my Na.D? I think you've inspired me to fight the good fight." Dr. Du'mas...now excited to recruit me, springs back out his chair, "Well...back when I got my degree it cost me around $250.000.00; but now with inflation, I bet it's a bit higher. No need to worry, those of us who graduated put together a college fund to pay for the education into this Niggatry to those we saw worthy, and son, although we just met, I can look into your soul and see...you're worthy!"

As if to hug me, he grabs me around my shoulder. I duck under him and make my way to the door. As I open it, I look back at this old, seventy-something White Man and smile, "You're soo full of shit! Enjoy your life Dr. Dumbass!"

As I make my way out of his office and onto the street, I reach for my phone and dial a number..."Whassup..."

"Is this Fa$e?"

"Whassup..."

"This is Jimmy. Jimmy Fisher from----" He cuts me off.

"Jimmy Fisher from Keokuk, Iowa. Yeah, I remember...Whassup?"

"I was down here in Atlanta, interviewing a self-proclaimed Niggaologist named Dr. Jameston Du'mas. After hours of listening to his bullshit, it finally came out that he went to *your* University. Is this true?"

Fa$e laughs..."If Trump can have Trump University, surely I can have a Fa$e university. What can I say, Jimmy, people need hope."

"Is it true you charged him, and everyone else two hundred fifty thousand dollars to receive their degree?"

"How you think I pay fo'dem nice ass cars in my driveway? Dope dealing...naw Jimmy from Keokuk, Iowa. I have been doin'dis shit since befo' Bankman, Holmes and all dem otha'cats. The only difference is...I don't need da'spotlight. Ya'see, I stay where I belong. I live according to my nature. It's when we ignore our nature, and do shit outside our instruction manual, life bends us ova'n fuck us. It's when we try ta'live bigger that our station in life, fucked up shit happens to us. So, me Jimmy... I let the Niggas have dis'shit. I'ma stay in'da background and roll how a real Nigga spose'ta roll. Slow and steady...da'sa lesson you should'a learned from the tortoise and the hare."

I can't even process it all! "Fa$e... you've given me a whole new outlook on life."

"Now it's time to start livin'life den...Jimmy from Keokuk, Iowa." Click...and just like that I'm...I don't even care anymore! I'm calling a taxi, and hopefully, it's the Woman who picked me up from the airport!

# Chapter 9:
# Lesson Learned

**<u>Several Weeks Later... (7:55 p.m.) Lesson Learned</u>**

After leaving the interview with Dr. Dumbass, I was left with the impression that "We the People" are delusional. In addition to our delusion, I think we've become numb to our duties as citizens of this Great country, especially as it pertains to the treatment or lack thereof when dealing with each other with a sense of humanity and civility. I discovered myself in a rush to conclude, yet something inside me tells me that if I rush, my conclusion will be strictly drawn from an emotional point of view. With all that I've learned these past few weeks, I think it's only apropos that I reach a conclusion based more so from the critical analytical analysis standpoint.

I decided to give myself a few weeks to process and reflect on all that had taken place; to rummage through all the emotions and thoughts that had engulfed my being these past few weeks. After weeks of contemplation, I think I finally understand why there's such a chasm between the perception of America and the reality of America. Meaning... Life, Liberty and the Pursuit of Happiness- and what that declaration means to those of us who live in America. Because to each of us (based on culture, tradition, upbringing, etc.), those words carry with us a different degree of hope.

I noticed after returning to my hometown, that my experience had changed me...evolved me in a sense. It is here, on a quiet, cool autumn evening that I find myself sitting on my front porch enjoying the familiar aromas of Keokuk, Iowa. It is here, now in this very moment in my life, that I discover myself, at home, yet feeling out-of-place and alone. As if I no longer belonged to this beautiful serene place I'd called home for the twenty-one years of my entire life! It was as if the past few weeks had left an indelible mark on my heart! I wondered what was it. Pity...guilt...anger...frustration...or just the fact that I discovered myself with a burning desire for more questions to be answered? Maybe it was the fact that immersing myself in someone else's lifestyle and not being judgmental, allowed me the precious opportunity to humble myself, and simply say, 'I see you and respect you.' So, what have I learned...

I've learned that, although I may not agree with someone else's lifestyle, it's best if I just try to understand the 'Why.' I once asked an aging, retiring reporter for a bit of parting wisdom, something to light the fire in my budding journalism career. She simply leaned back in her worn, faded leather chair, looked me square in my youthful eyes, smiled, and replied, "The best advice I could ever give anyone who desires a life well-lived is, never search for the answer...try instead to enjoy the journey that the burning questions of life will take you on." I never truly understood that, until this moment...

After weeks of meditating and mulling over the encounters I had with Fa$e and Dr. Dumbass, and even the conversation I had with the taxi driver in Atlanta...I finally realized what it means to be a Real Nigga. I don't know when or how it came to me, yet the epiphany sat on my chest as if I were bench pressing a thousand pounds, and in an instant, the weight just landed on my rib cage! It hit me...like a ton of bricks, splattering the cells of my brain, expanding my thoughts in ways unimaginable!

I now understand why Black People are hesitant when it comes to Western social structure(s) and societal rules; besides the glaring fact that they (Black People) had no stake in writing out these rules. To be quite honest...it's all bullshit! How so, you ask? Think about it...and I mean think about it and be honest with yourself. Those of us (White People) with the power-I mean structural, life-changing, generational wealth-building power desire the pleasures of Blackness. Yet we ostracize, vilify, emasculate, imprison and demonize all of what we perceive to be the negative that comes along with that Blackness!

We overindulge in the culture--food, dress, vernacular, hairstyles, music, and all the swag we can carry-all that makes being Black 'LIT'. We enjoy basking in the rhythm and the vibe; yet we minimize and/or discredit the pain that Black people went through (and still go through) to reach their levels of inner Greatness! It's like...we Desire the happy ending to the novel; yet we lack the Spiritual fortitude to suffer through the plot, nor do we have the mental strength to endure the climax.

We've chosen instead the path of least resistance. Turning our noses up to the struggle and the heartache of an entire Nation of Human Beings! While simultaneously ignoring the pain (that we as a White race have caused); pain that has been bequeathed to generations of innocent, unsuspecting Black souls!

We've chosen not to acknowledge the active role that 'We the People' have played in this mendacious plot to reign supreme 'by any means necessary!' "We The People" have become professionals at feigning innocence, washing our hands of the blood spilled as if we're Pontius Pilate presiding over the trial and execution of Jesus Christ! We've minimized our role in accepting that 'We the People' are the reason our country, this place we hold near and dear to our hearts, is the way it is in this day and age!

And this type of minimizing isn't unique to America. Due to our ignorance, this malicious mindset has penetrated and permeated the minds and hearts of Human Beings around the world. I'll give you a simple example, one that could be understood on a microcosmic level. Take an event like the Grammy's; a place where you're supposed to be recognized on the world stage for your talent towards bringing your culture to life. I recently watched a female reggae artist, who goes by the name Spice, get snubbed for a group out of Virginia named SOJA.

Now it may be harmless at first, however, delve deeper into what happened. A Jamaican-born female reggae artist got snubbed for an all-white group SOJA, in a category that was supposed to honor reggae artists! And that is just a simple example of what's happening on the microcosmic level! Take a moment and think about the macro...

Just imagine how many areas of life we (well-meaning White people) have finessed our way into, while simultaneously excluding another group of people. Think of all the laws we've created; laws that benefit us and our progeny (blue-collar crime and punishment vs. the law for those we deem incorrigible). Think of all the manipulation that we've put in place...so that we can maintain...power. Power over land...power over products... the power of property... the power of Human Beings... the power of the future! We've placed ourselves in the greatest positions on earth...all by executing Nigga shit to its fullest potential!

If you think I'm being hyperbolic...I'll give you just a few examples:

-1492 (We already know what Christopher Columbus did to the Arawak Natives. If you don't know, read the journals of his discovery of the Americas.)

-1619 (White People brought Africans to the Americas, not as explorers, but as slaves. Yet again...I don't have to give you-the reader-a dissertation on what happened in the following centuries.)

-1776 (We declared ourselves a free Nation, stating, 'We hold these truths to be self-evident, that all MEN are created equal, that they are endowed by their Creator with certain unalienable Rights, that among these are Life, Liberty and the pursuit of Happiness."-yet we wrote Africans (slaves) into the very same Declaration of Independence and United States Constitution as 3/5 the of a Human Being 'property').

-1865 (Once slavery ended, we created a 'Reconstruction' period, a time in which equality would finally reign for all; yet we abandoned that ideology and allowed disgruntled White Southerners (Ku Klux Klan) to terrorize, lynch, rape, murder, and once again dehumanize those Africans who were fresh out of slavery, as well as their descendants...for another 100 years!!!

G.I Bill was established on June 22, 1944 (Uncle Sam asked that every able-bodied Man join the war efforts. In return, congress passed the G.I. Bill. This bill gave money (most noticeably, school grants and housing grants) to veterans returning home from the war. The only catch was...this money (OPPORTUNITY) was not afforded to those Women and Men of color who fought bravely-enduring those untold horrors and returned home.)

-1965 (African-Americans are still fighting for their basic Human Rights. Yet they settle for a law that claims to grant them civil rights!) Think about that...asking to be treated as Human, and being denied; so instead, you settle for just being treated with civility!

-Present-Day (Unarmed Black Men being gunned down by those who are sworn to serve and protect. Black neighborhoods crumble from lack of resources. School-to-prison pipeline created, specializing in sending more young Black Men to prison.)

And this is just me naming a few! I'm pretty sure a historian could give you a greater in-depth understanding of the atrocities that have been endured by Women and Men of Color. It's as if 'We the People' (White People) have adopted the ideology of Malthusian Theory; in which People of Color are being systematically kept at the bottom, in a perpetual 'struggle for existence' mode. And this has been the status quo for the past five hundred plus years! Just knowing what I know, and having an opportunity to experience a world opposite of the safety, comfort, and supremacy of my world, I can now empathize with the built-up resentment and mistrust of Fa$e and those in his world. I can understand their fuck the world mentality!

Stumbling upon the Nigga Ball was an eye-opener. Meeting Fa$e was a Godsend! I learned a very valuable life lesson while riding along with Fa$e. What made him Real was the fact that he was free! He believed he had earned his freedom, by simply being born into this world. He knew that his freedom provided him with a plethora of choices in life; and with every choice, he was willing to accept and honor the results. He understood his position in this world, and therefore he understood why his freedom was so precious!

Why he lived the life the Founding Fathers declared that every Man and Woman were endowed with? He lived the life of a modern-day American samurai. Whether we (society) agree with his lifestyle or not, Fa$e and those like him, took what scraps America gave and created a viable, breathing, tangible American Dream for themselves! They didn't cry and blame the White Man nor did they give up on their hopes and dreams. They simply said this world and everything in it is theirs for the taking! No different than Rockefeller, J.P Morgan, Gates, Bezos, or any other Dreamer.

Something else that I admire about Fa$e and his world. He and his associates stuck to a set of codes and ethics that, although unwritten in the books or laws of the American judicial system; these codes and ethics remained etched in their hearts and minds as if they were as powerful, if not more powerful than the Ten Commandments. In addition to that, from the time I was in their presence, they honored their codes, their ethics, and their way of life. They respected their lifestyle...as if it were their religion.

I witnessed firsthand what Men looked like and how they operated. Fa$e could be said to be a lot of things...but in my time with him, I can honestly say, he wasn't a coward. He spoke with authority and truth. In many ways, he spoke with Love, yet it was a Love that you could only know if you lived in those trenches! Those Men and Women I met while riding along with Fa$e deserve the most prestigious award I could ever give...and that is...the award for being Honorable, Respectable, Loyal Human Beings.

Now juxtapose Fa$e and his associates with the lifestyles of the people that won the awards at the Nigga Ball. The same can't be said for the Hitlers of the world. Nor can it be said about the Elizabeth Holmes; the R.Kellys'; the Trumps; and Sam Bankmans' of the world. They are the true cowards of our time, yet we reward them with the spoils of life. "We as a society should rethink what's real and what's fake, or simply put what's honorable and what's dishonorable. I can honestly say I grew up reporting this story. Not as a Man, or even a reporter for that matter. Something inside me grew...evolved...and experienced...Yeah...ole Jimmy Fisher from Keokuk, Iowa; my nuts finally dropped. Who knew I'd learn so much from The Realist Nigga...

Phone rings...I notice it's Fa$e phone number. "Hello...how have you been Fa$e?"

"Is'dis Jimmy?"

"Yes...who is this?"

"Wha'chu mean who is dis? Dis'da bitch dat swallowed all six yo inches at da house party da other night! You don't remember my voice."

"How could I, we never spoke."

"Well...now we speak'n. I'm just call'n ta'tell you...I'm pregnant, and we gone have a lil light-skinned

Stephen Curry! Whassup Baby daddy!!! O-kurrrrrrrrrr!!!"

My head drops into my lap, and I hear a male's voice on the other end of the phone. "Jimmy from Keokuk, Iowa...don't trip, every Nigga got a crazy baby mama!!!" I hold my head up and smile...Fuck it...

To Be Continued...

# Glossary

1.) **Nigga-**[A euphemism, although delusional, self-inflicted and self-destructive] 1. Derived from the word, Nigger, the word Nigga was created sometime in the early 1900's by the descendants of slaves, who sought, presumably to normalize and take power from the originators of the word. 2. A term of endearment, used by one ignorant Human Being to describe his/her contemporaries.

2.) **Niggatry-**1. The term encompasses the length, breadth, depth and height of ignorance.

3.) **Niggaism-**1. The philosophy, doctrine and creed of a 'Nigga.'

4.) **Niggerish-**1. Of or belonging to the class of Niggas (whether it be through one's words, acts and/or deeds.) 2. Having the undesirable quality of a Nigga.

5.) **Niggadome-**1. The immersion of one's entire mind (thought process) into the way of life of being ignorant. 2. The thought process that leads to a Human Being breathing, thinking and therefore living the life of a 'Nigga.'

6.) **Niggaologist-**1. One who is *trained* and certified in the science of being and understanding a 'Nigga'. 2. The Science that deals with the lifestyle of ignorant Human Beings, as well as their way of processing life.

7.) **Niggacide-**1. The deliberate and systematic destruction of one's self (mind), peers and community through acts of ignorance (i.e., gun violence, drugs, lack of education, etc.) 2. A 'Nigga' who inflicts harm upon her/himself or another Human Being; causing chaos, destruction or death.

8.) **Nigga-aide-**1. The propaganda that is spewed amongst Niggas, that enables them to captivate an unsuspecting audience.

9.) **Niggalicious-**1. The sensational gratifying of one's senses while immersed into the ideology of being a Nigga. 2. The act of indulging in an event (or events) that, at their core are Niggerish; yet finding a certain amount of pleasure and/or enjoyment in such an event. 3. To commit an act that is, of its essence Niggerish; and still be in a state of bliss.

10.) **Nocturnal Niggas-**1. Niggas who, under the cover of darkness, have perfected the art of thriving by any means necessary (i.e., robbing, selling drugs, tricking, stealing, etc.) 2. A term that defines an ignorant person who does their 'work' during the midnight hours. 3. One who is comfortable, and at home, when surrounded by darkness and confusion. 4. Ignorant people who lurk in the darkness of night.

11.) **Niggaroid-**1. When a White person has a traumatic experience (one that is life-altering); and this experience is usually reserved for a Black person. When a white person diverts from their 'normal suburbian-safe' mentality; and converts to a 'hood mentality.'

Somewhere in Southeast Iowa (in the Iowa State Penitentiary)

Man picks up prison phone...

*(Operator speaking) Press 1 for English...*

*The time is 2:44 p.m....*

*Called parties are now required to listen to the entire message before making a selection. Please be patient...*

*Press 1 to place a call...*

*Please enter you pin number, followed by the pound sign...*

*To place a call press 1...*

*Your account balance is $46.89...*

*For calls within the United States, Canada and the Caribbean, please enter the area code followed by the seven-digit number...*

*(PHONE RINGING... PHONE RINGING...PHONE RINGING)* Someone picks up.

*(Operator speaking) You have a call at no expense to you from, 'Omar'; an inmate at the Iowa State Penitentiary, in Fort Madison, Iowa. You must listen to the entire message before entering a selection. To accept the call, press 5. To refuse the call, hang up now. To block this call and all future calls, press 9. You may enter a selection now...*

# The Interview:

Interviewer: Hello...is this Mr. Omar Wilkins?

Mr. Wilkins: Why yes, it is.

Interviewer: Good Morning Mr.Wilkins. How are you today?

Mr. Wilkins: Beautiful...Life loves me and I'm loving Her back!

Interviewer: That's an amazing outlook considering you've been incarcerated for the past 21+ years. How do you do it?

Mr. Wilkins: One year, one month, one day, one hour, one minute, one second at a time. I've learned to live in the moment. Stop wishing for tomorrow and stop reliving yesterday! Because yesterday is gone and tomorrow may never come. So, all I have is this moment. If I can live in this moment and make it count, my regrets will become fewer and fewer and my tomorrow will become brighter and brighter.

Interviewer: That's a positive outlook on things. Before we start this interview, are there any questions you may have for me, or is there anything off-limits?

Mr. Wilkins: No... You can ask whatever it is you think your reader may want to know, and I'll answer honestly. I'm an open book, so I stay as transparent as possible.

Interviewer: (Interview begins) Before we begin today, I'd like to take this moment to introduce my guest, Mr. Omar Wilkins. Mr. Wilkins is the author of the new book titled: The Art of the (am I allowed to say the word) (affirmative head nod) Nigga...An In-depth Understanding of the Inner Workings of Niggas, Niggaism, and Niggadome. He is also an Incarcerated Man, serving a life sentence at the Iowa State Penitentiary. Thank you for joining us today!

Mr. Wilkins: Why thank you for inviting me to speak on your platform. I must say, I am as delighted to be here as you are to have me.

Interviewer: First question, why am I speaking to you on a collect call from the Iowa State Prison?

Mr. Wilkins: Well... let's just say that in my earlier years, I indulged in the lifestyle of a Nigga and this has been my reward. But to put it more clearly, when I was 18, I was tried and convicted for the death of an innocent Man.

Interviewer: If you don't mind me asking, could you go into a little more detail?

Mr. Wilkins: Sure. When I was 16, I started coming to Iowa to sell drugs. I would make my runs back and forth, hustling as we called it. Well...fast forward two years later (and a plethora of Nigga shit in between). On one of my trips up here, we got into an altercation with a Man, and I ended up taking his life. Did I mean to? No. But the State of Iowa doesn't see the events of that tragic night as I do. So, a trial ensued and I was found guilty. All of this is on the internet. Although the story may differ a bit, the facts are solid: An innocent Man lost his life and I was the cause. Some Nigga shit took place and it all fell on my shoulders. Once it happens, there's no need to cry. As you'll learn from the book, Real Niggas don't complain.

Interviewer: So, are you a Real 'N'?

Mr. Wilkins: At that point in my life, yes, I was.

Interviewer: Okay...speaking of the book. As I read through your best-selling book, I must say that my mind was reading what seemed like a thousand miles a second! My jaws couldn't remain closed, and my eyes were bulging out of my head, this book is not only intense, and it's written in such a gritty, intelligent way! I must ask you, why...why such an in-depth, gritty, eye-opening, jarring plunge into a topic that has caused so much pain and tragedy; not just in America, but all over the world? Why would you even begin to write a book and discuss such a topic as the essence of a Nigga?

Mr. Wilkins: The simple answer is because the world and lifestyle of a Real Nigga is gritty, as well as intelligent! The question that I think should be asked isn't 'Why did I...' The question the world should be asking is, 'How did we come to the point of making Niggaism a socially acceptable part of our society?' I only took the time to sit down and articulate, which is witnessed all day every day in our society.

Whether it be reality TV, our work environment, our neighborhoods, or even in our dealings with each other, or even the highest office in government. I think it's time we accept the FACT that being a Nigga has transcended a race of people; a genre of music, a certain neighborhood, or even a specific continent, for that matter! Why...I would go as far as to even proclaim that being a Nigga has become a badge of honor! Just look around you, and if you understand the term, 'Nigga' and can separate it from its origin word, 'Nigger' then you'll begin to have your eyes opened to the acceptance of Niggatry.

Interviewer: Wow...fascinating!!! Before we delve into the degrees of Niggas, I think it would be enlightening if you were to give the audience an overview of the definition of Nigga and how it has come to differ from Nigger.

Mr. Wilkins: Sure...well I created the definition of Nigga, just thinking about how cool and socially acceptable being a Nigga has become. In addition, I traced its roots back to Antebellum (before the U.S. Civil War of 1861); so that those who are neophytes in this area can gain a better understanding of just how transcendent the word has become. My definition of Nigga is: [A euphemism, although delusionally self-inflicted and self-destructive] 1. Derived from the word, Nigger, the word Nigga was created sometime in the early 1900s by the descendants of slaves, who sought, presumably to normalize and take power from the originators of the word. 2. The term encompasses the breadth and depth of the ignorance, stagnation, regression; as well as the corrosive ideology of what it means to be an outcast of Hu-man-ity.

3. A term of endearment, used by one ignorant Human Being to describe his/her contemporaries.

Interviewer: Now...for the viewers' sake, let's delve a bit further into each definition. You describe the word, 'Nigga' as a 'euphemism'; as well as 'delusional and self-destructive'. Could you please expound upon those two descriptions?

Mr. Wilkins: Of course, my first thought every time I hear the word Nigga blasted from the lips of a Human Being; whether it be a movie, a song, a book, or an actual person speaking is, 'Well...that's a cooler way to call someone a worthless slave!' Yet, the term has been accepted by descendants of slaves and utilized openly and freely in their everyday lives. The word Nigga has become commercialized, and therefore socially acceptable. Now just because something is normalized and socially acceptable, doesn't make it right and/or responsible. Has any derogatory term used to annihilate the Jewish people become socially acceptable or normalized? Has any term that was used while the imprisonment of Japanese in internment camps during the War become popularized?

No...and you know why because any Nation of people understands that for a subjugated and emasculated Nation of people to become truly free and therefore sovereign; that nation must denounce and destroy all remnants of that which held them in such a state! Any Nation of people who can't seem to understand and grasp that concept must be mentally suffering, therefore delusional, and consequently self-destructive to the causes and advancement of their Nation and Its causes!

Interviewer: Powerful thoughts Mr. Wilkins, have you given any thought as to why a Nation (presuming, we're speaking on Black people in America) would allow such a word to haunt them and their social status, right up until this very moment?

Mr. Wilkins: It is often said that ignorance is bliss, yet throughout my years of experience, I've found that ignorance is sad! Take the second and third definitions, nowhere in those are words such as gleeful, giddy, happy, and playful. Nothing about being immersed in the world of Niggadome makes you genuinely blissful!

As Human Beings, being part of Hu-man-ity as a whole, we have bestowed upon us the ability to transcend those circumstances which hold us in states of mental ineptness. Yet, to stay in a place of chaos and delusion, willingly I might add, is sad, at least in my opinion of my life experiences.

Interviewer: You just used the word 'Niggadome'. Throughout the book, there are words that you created that are derived from the word Nigga. What was the impetus for this train of thought?

Mr. Wilkins: Well there are a few words that I have created because with any lifestyle you have to understand that it (the lifestyle) becomes somewhat of a religion. In addition, we must understand that those who immerse themselves into that lifestyle; and by immerse, I mean going all in into the doctrine, philosophy, and creed of that lifestyle are in essence...zealots. This means that lifestyle comes alive within those who immerse themselves in it and with that it (the lifestyle) will take on a lingo of its own.

With that being said, I expressed to you earlier that being a Nigga is a way of life, a way of life that has transcended race, sex, generation, and class. If you look at my original definition of the word Nigga, you will begin to understand that that definition can easily describe anyone; from the kid who wants to be cool, to the politician who steals from his/her constituency. I know I got away from the original question, with that being said, some of the terms that I have coined and defined in the book are Niggaism, Niggadome, Niggalicious, Niggatry, Niggaroid, Nigga-Aide, and Niggaologist. Each of these words has its root in the ideology of what it means to be a Nigga. Yet each word branching off into its meaning...taking on a life of its own if you will...

**Interviewer:** I just find it quite remarkable how you masterfully weaved it all together. Tell me...why Jimmy Fisher from Keokuk, Iowa; why not Derrick or Iesha from, say...Atlanta?

**Mr. Wilkins:** Because Derrick or Iesha couldn't make you, the audience believes this story. You see... to make this narrative (as well as this journey) believable for the reader, it had to come from a character removed from the world of a Nigga. I wrote this book specifically for the neophytes who have questions about what it means to be a Real Nigga. Just imagine...you not knowing how to...redo your kitchen, yet you have the desire to learn. What would you do? You would first research how to redo your kitchen. You would go to the professionals and look them over, see what their websites say, and from there you'd have a pretty good idea of who to learn from. Jimmy did the same thing. He went to the Nigga Ball, and from listening to the crowd there, he got an idea of who he should be interviewing. This story can only be told from the viewpoint of a 21-year-old white boy from Keokuk, Iowa who's never been in trouble, and has only dated one girl; yet he has the credentials (by being a journalist) to tell this story. In addition...he doesn't go in with any preconceived notions about what is or isn't a Real Nigga. He's just a sponge, soaking up the information and disseminating said information to the public.

*(Operator: You have one minute remaining.)*

**Interviewer:** I'm so excited for the world to get a glimpse of the lifestyle of, the New Age Nigga...What's next for you Mr. Wilkins?

**Mr. Wilkins:** Well, I'm hoping to have a plethora of children's book series out by this time next year (Detroit's Finest; The Adventures of Li-Lo-Li and Omo, part 2; Justa). As well as part two and three of The Art of The Nigga, and... well let's just say: BLACK N.A.T.O...

**Interviewer:** Before I get swept into all these projects, my producers are signaling for me to wrap this up, thank you for your time and your candor.

# A Conversation Between A Man and a Nigga

"Wha'dup my Nigga?"

"I'm not your Nigga! I'm a Man, and there's a great chasm between the two."

"Oh yeah...shit I'own see no difference. Mothafuckas holdin you down, just like they holdin me down."

"No one is holding me down! As a matter fact I Am Master of my Fate and the Captain of my Destiny. I'm a Father, a Human Being, a Contributor to my community, an asset to anyone and anything I involve myself in. Whoever the 'they' are that you speak of as holding you down...that's bullshit! You're holding yourself down. Jobs are plentiful, America is replete with opportunities for Men and Women alike. It is the Niggas who have placed themselves in a state of perpetual servitude."

"Man...all dat shit sounds good. What you some type a Muslim, cause own'know bout you, but real Niggas got it bad out here!"

"You got it bad because you've placed yourself into the station of a 'Real Nigga' with your actions; or I should say your inaction. Yeah...as a Man I struggle. Yet no life is easy. However, I have acquired the tools to masterfully navigate this world. I may not be a millionaire; however I know and understand that I have what it takes to ascertain wealth! I have Ideas, Faith, Desire, a Will that's unstoppable and I am persistent when it comes to capturing the objects of my Desire. Real Men are flourishing in this world! You see...we have figured out how to harness the Universal Force that surrounds us, thereby truly taking our rightful stations as Lord of this Creation."

"Damn...that's some deep shit! I mean...I never thought about nothing dat deep. His you get to some like that?"

"By thinking!!! You see, when a Man makes the conscious decision to Think, He'll begin to store those thoughts within his Mind. Those thoughts, when in line with Universal Laws, will cause a Man to insert Himself into the events of the world, thereby bringing about results that were in line with His thoughts. Men are by Nature Thinkers! Masters of their Fate...in such a way that no one can stop them from pursuing and conquering the objects they desire."

"How do I begin this journey to becoming a Man?"

"First you must realize that within you is everything you need to place yourself amongst the ranks of Men! No one, not your Mama, your Woman, the Man, no amount of money can make you a Man! You must face your trials head on, overcoming buffetings of every kind. Yet with every defeat you'll gain wisdom and self-awareness. And with every victory you'll gain humility, Love, Faith and the Courage to continue onward and upward! This journey will allow you to harness your abilities."

"Ables...what does that mean?"

"Able simply means are you honorABLE? Are you reliABLE? Are you dependABLE? Are you capABLE? Are you admirABLE? Are you trustABLE? Are you respectABLE? Are you ABLE-bodied? Are you viABLE? Are you understandABLE? Are you knowledgeABLE? Are you stABLE? Are you adaptABLE? Are you pliABLE? Are you adjustABLE? Are you quantifiABLE? Are you reasonABLE? Are you availABLE? Are you approachABLE? Are you unshakeABLE? Are you evolvABLE? Are you trainABLE? Are you huggABLE? Are you trustABLE? Are you loveABLE? If you truly have the desire to transcend from a Nigga to a Man, all you have to do is THINK DIFFERENT!"

What does it mean to be a REAL Nigga in the year 2023? How does a REAL Nigga think...operate...and conduct their business on a day-to-day basis? Who are the REAL Niggas and where do they reside? These are the questions that Jimmy Fisher (a 21-year-old White freelance reporter from Keokuk, Iowa) discovered himself in search of.

Join Jimmy Fisher as he delves into the world of REAL Niggas. Witness as he encounters 'Fa$e'; a well-known REAL Nigga. Jimmy Fisher and Mr. Fa$e go on an adventure that could only be described as...enlightening! And lastly...Jimmy Fisher indulges the ignorance of Jameston Du'mas (a self-proclaimed Niggaologist.) Be prepared to have you mind blown on what it takes to be a REAL Nigga in the year 2023.